Clay County Public
Library

STAR WARS®

INFINITIES
RETURN OF THE JEDI™

VOLUME THREE

SCRIPT
ADAM GALLARDO

PENCILS
RYAN BENJAMIN

INKS
SALEEM CRAWFORD

COLORS
JOEL BENJAMIN

LETTERING
MICHAEL DAVID THOMAS

COVER ART
RODOLFO MIGLIARI

Lando Calrissian, Chewbacca, and Princess Leia tracked the bounty hunter Boba Fett to a rendezvous with Imperial officers. Fett was killed in the ensuing battle, but Leia and the others were able to rescue Han Solo, still frozen in carbonite.

On Dagobah, where he had gone to consult with the ghosts of Yoda and Obi-Wan Kenobi, Luke Skywalker learned that Leia is his sister—and that both of them are the children of Darth Vader.

But when Luke attempted to depart and rejoin the Rebel fleet gathered near Sullust, he was caught by the Empire, barely able to transmit a warning to Leia before being taken prisoner by Darth Vader.

THE *STAR WARS INFINITIES* SERIES ASKS THE QUESTION: WHAT IF ONE THING HAPPENED DIFFERENTLY FROM WHAT WE SAW IN THE CLASSIC FILMS?

Spotlight

DARK HORSE COMICS

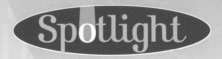

Visit us at www.abdopublishing.com

Reinforced library bound edition published in 2011 by Spotlight, a division of the ABDO Group, 8000 West 78th Street, Edina, Minnesota 55439. Spotlight produces high-quality reinforced library bound editions for schools and libraries. Published by agreement with Dark Horse Comics, Inc., and Lucasfilm Ltd.

Printed in the United States of America, North Mankato, Minnesota.
102010
012011
This book contains at least 10% recycled materials.

Library of Congress Cataloging-in-Publication Data

Gallardo, Adam.
Return of the Jedi / script, Adam Gallardo ; art, Ryan Benjamin. -- Reinforced library bound ed.
p. cm. -- (Star wars. Infinities)
ISBN 978-1-59961-853-1 (vol. 1) -- ISBN 978-1-59961-854-8 (vol. 2) -- ISBN 978-1-59961-855-5 (vol. 3) -- ISBN 978-1-59961-856-2 (vol. 4)
1. Graphic novels. [1. Graphic novels. 2. Science fiction.] I. Benjamin, Ryan, ill. II. Title.
PZ7.7.G35Ret 2011
741.5'973--dc22

2010020250

Spotlight

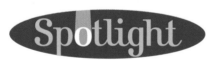

All Spotlight books have reinforced library bindings and are manufactured in the United States of America.

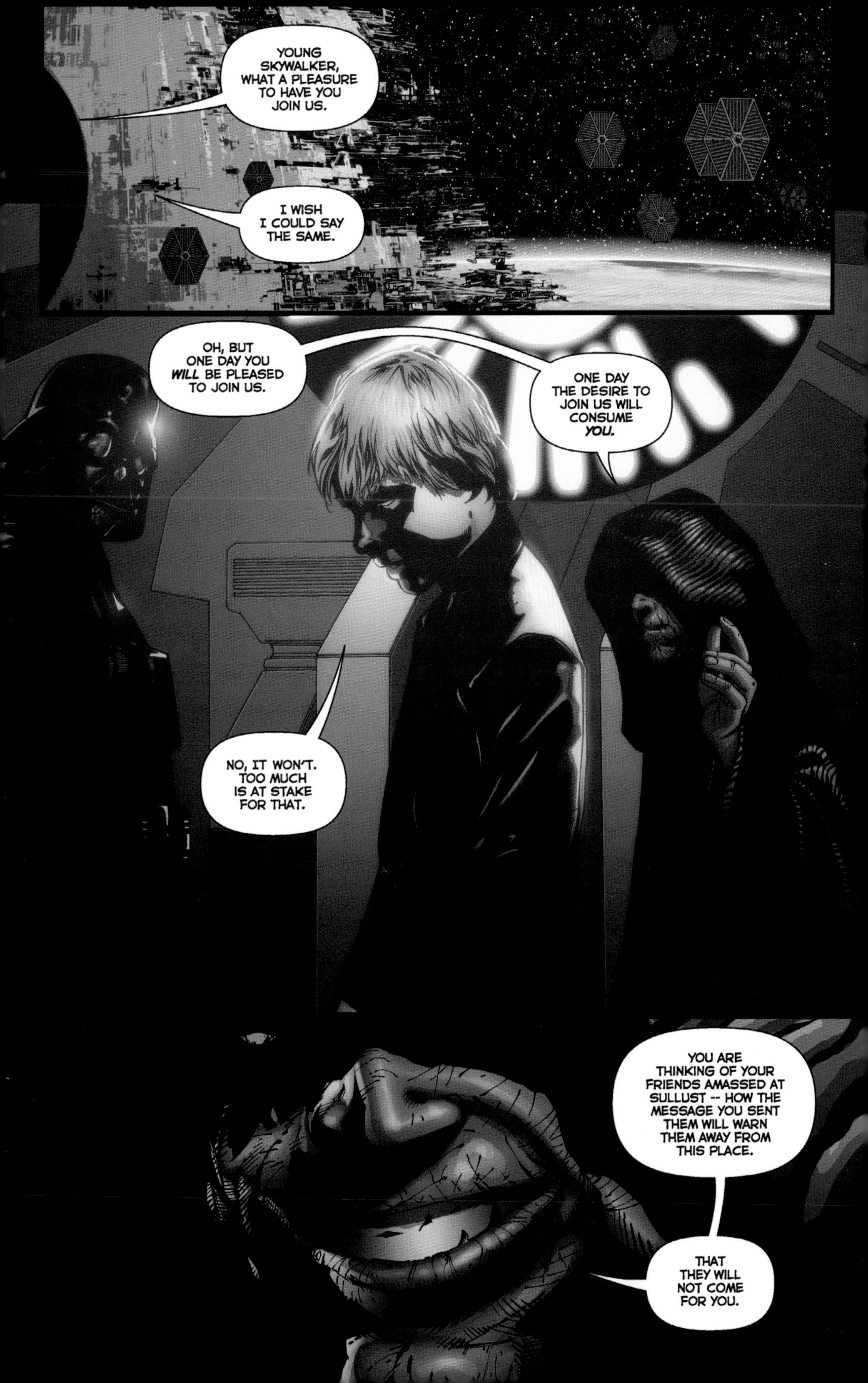

YOUNG SKYWALKER, WHAT A PLEASURE TO HAVE YOU JOIN US.
I WISH I COULD SAY THE SAME.
OH, BUT ONE DAY YOU *WILL* BE PLEASED TO JOIN US.
ONE DAY THE DESIRE TO JOIN US WILL CONSUME *YOU.*
NO, IT WON'T. TOO MUCH IS AT STAKE FOR THAT.
YOU ARE THINKING OF YOUR FRIENDS AMASSED AT SULLUST -- HOW THE MESSAGE YOU SENT THEM WILL WARN THEM AWAY FROM THIS PLACE.
THAT THEY WILL NOT COME FOR YOU.

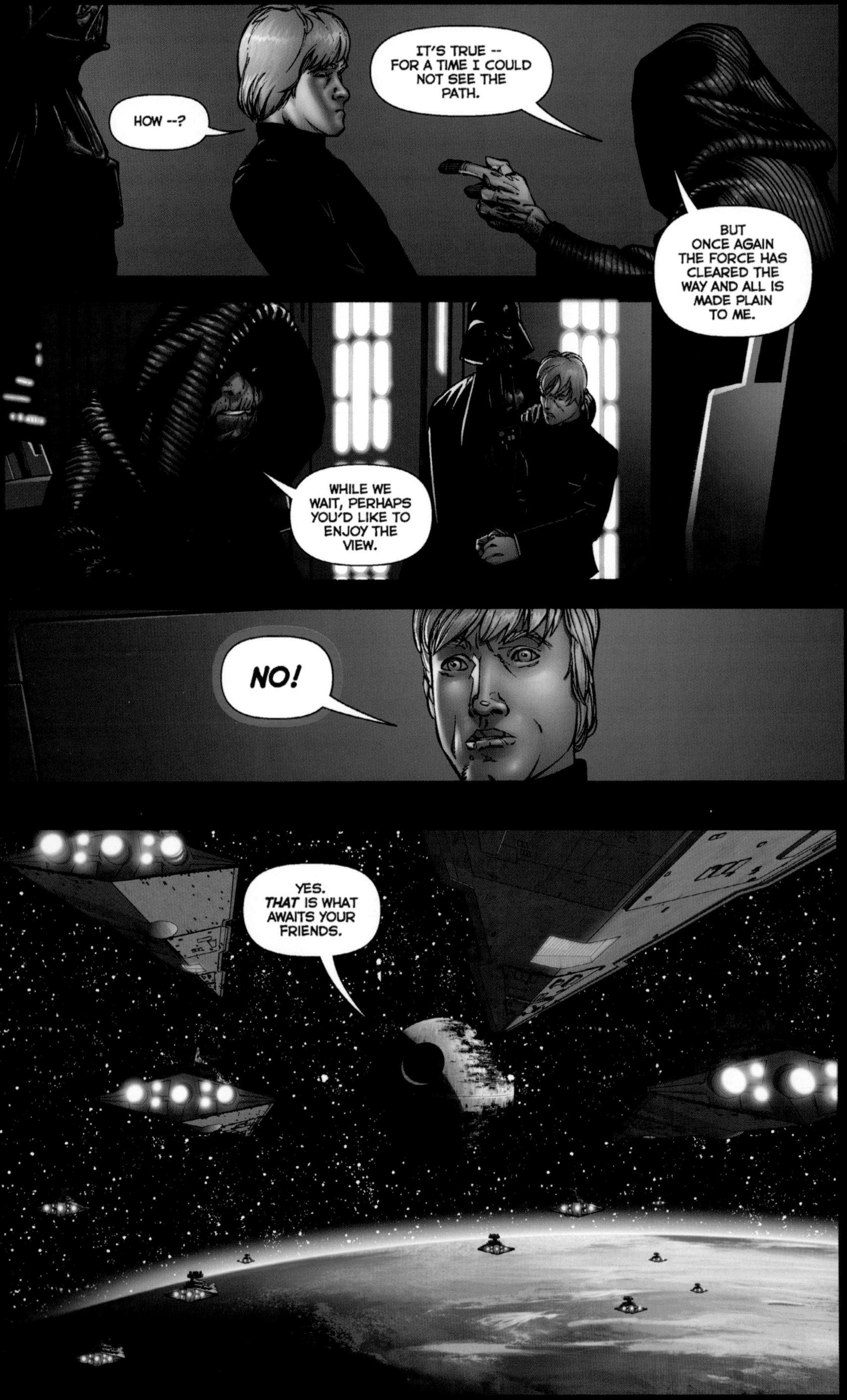
HOW --?
IT'S TRUE -- FOR A TIME I COULD NOT SEE THE PATH.
BUT ONCE AGAIN THE FORCE HAS CLEARED THE WAY AND ALL IS MADE PLAIN TO ME.
WHILE WE WAIT, PERHAPS YOU'D LIKE TO ENJOY THE VIEW.
NO!
YES. THAT IS WHAT AWAITS YOUR FRIENDS.

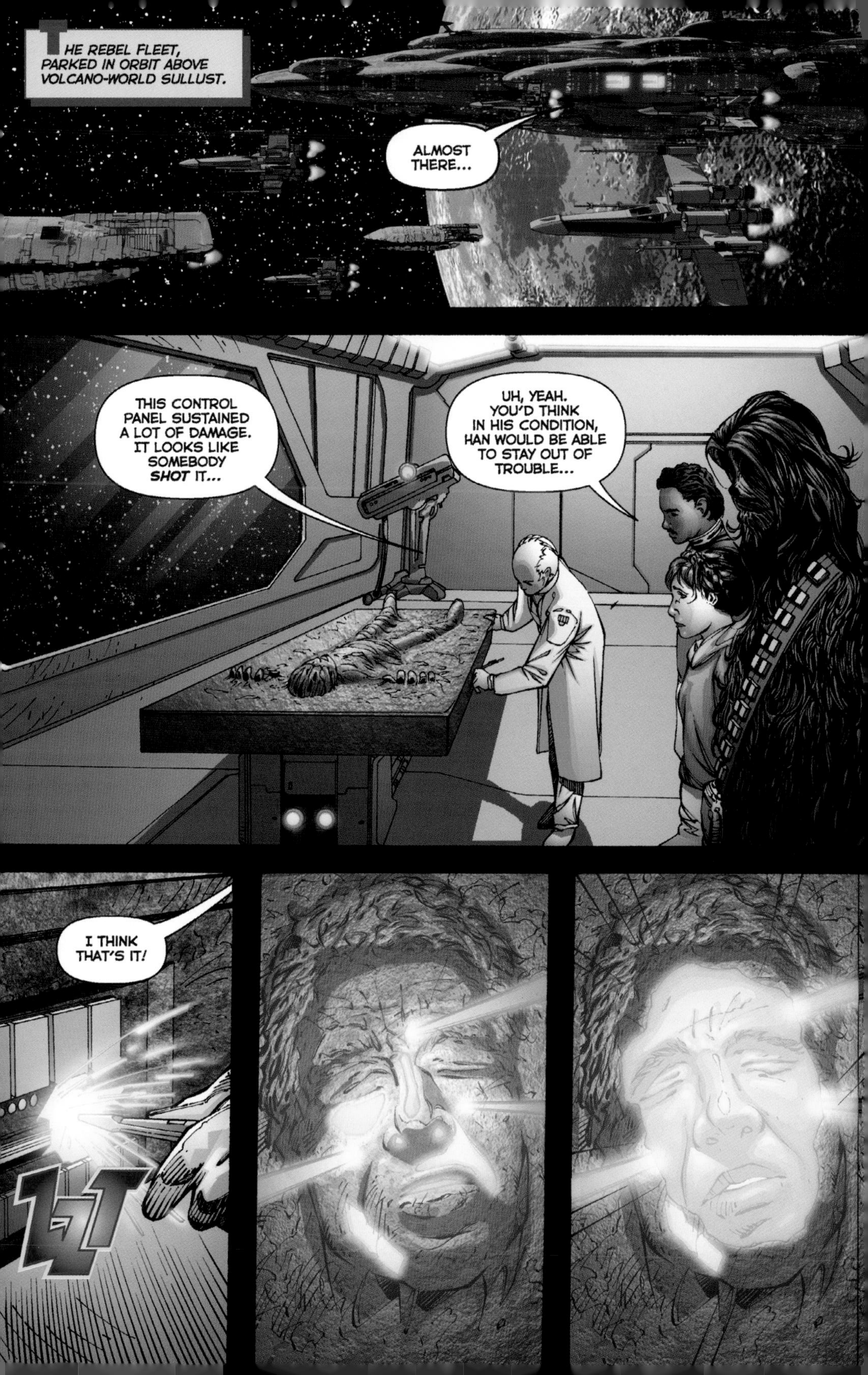
THE REBEL FLEET, PARKED IN ORBIT ABOVE VOLCANO-WORLD SULLUST.
ALMOST THERE...
THIS CONTROL PANEL SUSTAINED A LOT OF DAMAGE. IT LOOKS LIKE SOMEBODY SHOT IT...
UH, YEAH. YOU'D THINK IN HIS CONDITION, HAN WOULD BE ABLE TO STAY OUT OF TROUBLE...
I THINK THAT'S IT!
ZZT

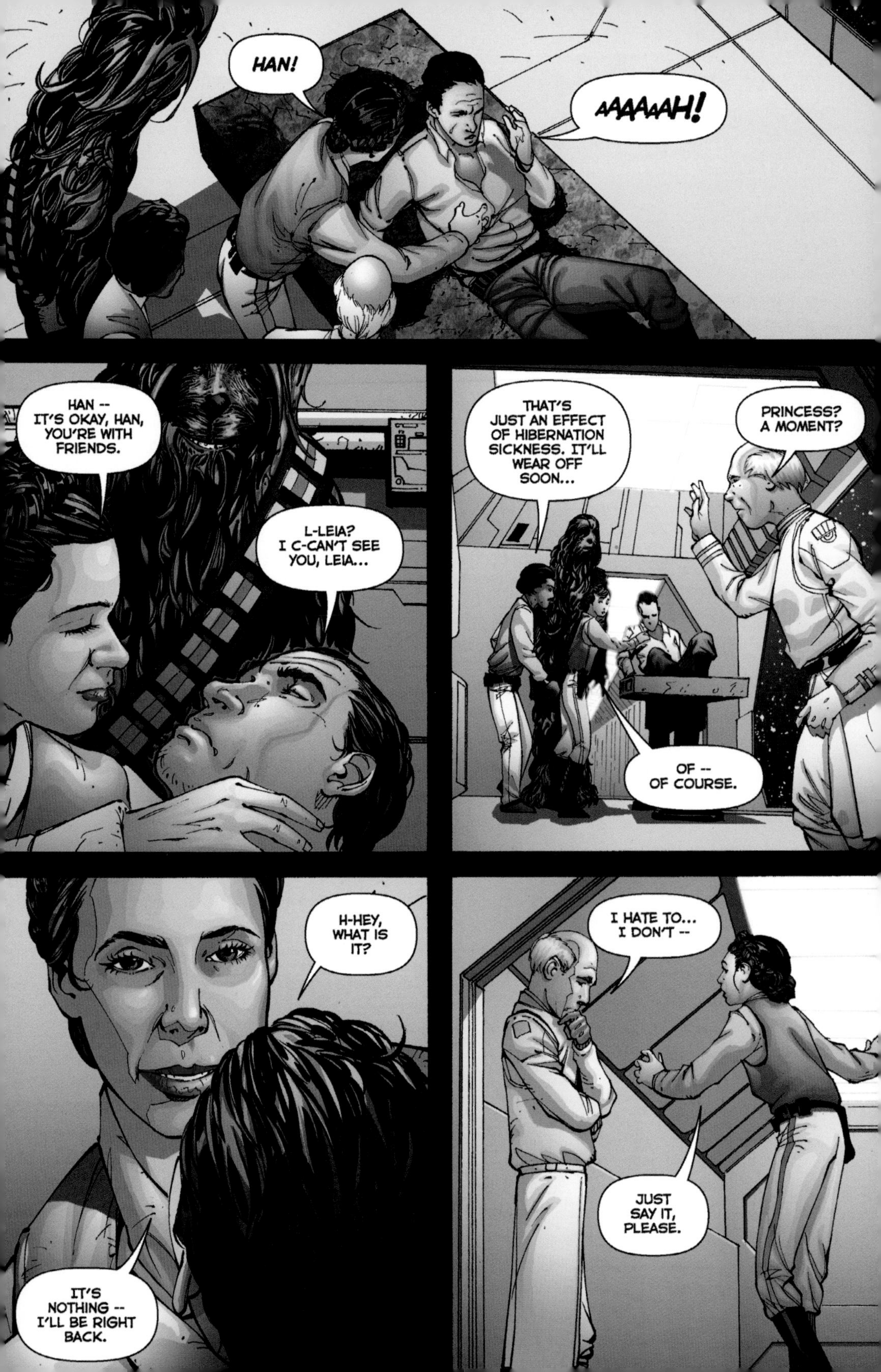
HAN!
AAAAAAH!
HAN -- IT'S OKAY, HAN, YOU'RE WITH FRIENDS.
L-LEIA? I C-CAN'T SEE YOU, LEIA...
THAT'S JUST AN EFFECT OF HIBERNATION SICKNESS. IT'LL WEAR OFF SOON...
PRINCESS? A MOMENT?
OF -- OF COURSE.
H-HEY, WHAT IS IT?
IT'S NOTHING -- I'LL BE RIGHT BACK.
I HATE TO... I DON'T --
JUST SAY IT, PLEASE.

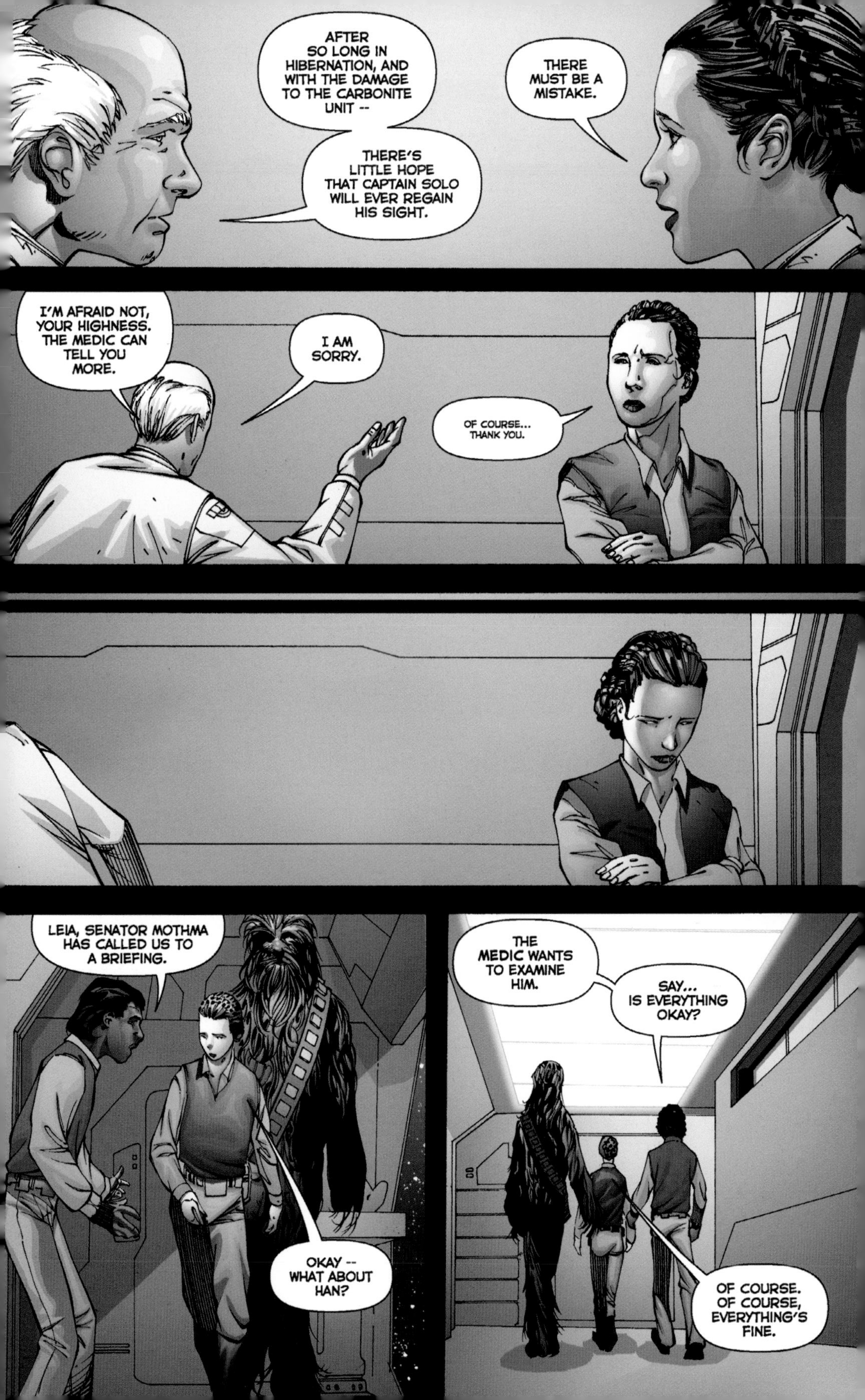

AFTER SO LONG IN HIBERNATION, AND WITH THE DAMAGE TO THE CARBONITE UNIT --
THERE'S LITTLE HOPE THAT CAPTAIN SOLO WILL EVER REGAIN HIS SIGHT.
THERE MUST BE A MISTAKE.
I'M AFRAID NOT, YOUR HIGHNESS. THE MEDIC CAN TELL YOU MORE.
I AM SORRY.
OF COURSE... THANK YOU.
LEIA, SENATOR MOTHMA HAS CALLED US TO A BRIEFING.
OKAY -- WHAT ABOUT HAN?
THE MEDIC WANTS TO EXAMINE HIM.
SAY... IS EVERYTHING OKAY?
OF COURSE. OF COURSE, EVERYTHING'S FINE.

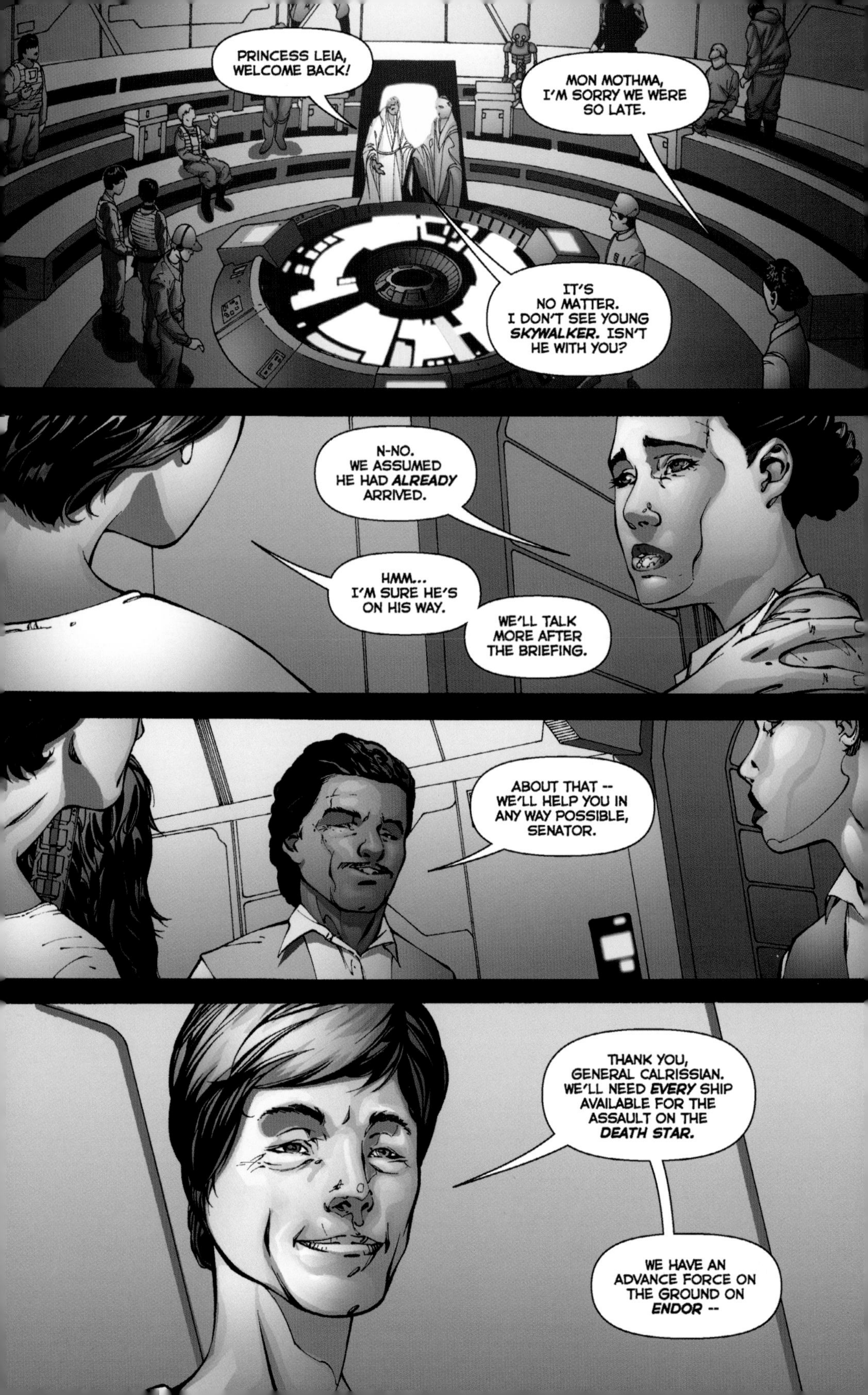
PRINCESS LEIA, WELCOME BACK!
MON MOTHMA, I'M SORRY WE WERE SO LATE.
IT'S NO MATTER. I DON'T SEE YOUNG SKYWALKER. ISN'T HE WITH YOU?
N-NO. WE ASSUMED HE HAD ALREADY ARRIVED.
HMM... I'M SURE HE'S ON HIS WAY.
WE'LL TALK MORE AFTER THE BRIEFING.
ABOUT THAT -- WE'LL HELP YOU IN ANY WAY POSSIBLE, SENATOR.
THANK YOU, GENERAL CALRISSIAN. WE'LL NEED EVERY SHIP AVAILABLE FOR THE ASSAULT ON THE DEATH STAR.
WE HAVE AN ADVANCE FORCE ON THE GROUND ON ENDOR --

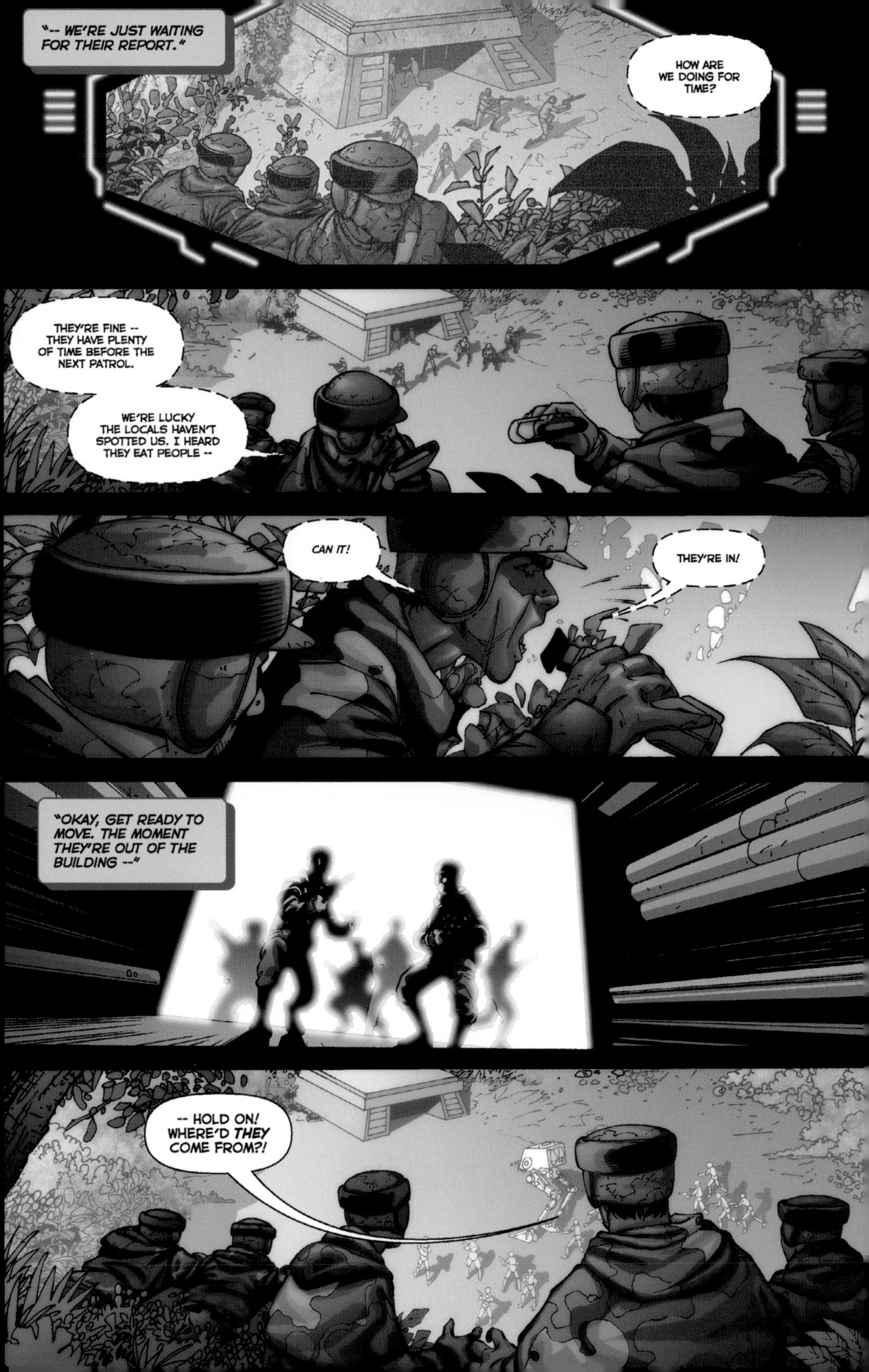
"-- WE'RE JUST WAITING FOR THEIR REPORT."
HOW ARE WE DOING FOR TIME?
THEY'RE FINE -- THEY HAVE PLENTY OF TIME BEFORE THE NEXT PATROL.
WE'RE LUCKY THE LOCALS HAVEN'T SPOTTED US. I HEARD THEY EAT PEOPLE --
CAN IT!
THEY'RE IN!
"OKAY, GET READY TO MOVE. THE MOMENT THEY'RE OUT OF THE BUILDING --"
-- HOLD ON! WHERE'D THEY COME FROM?!

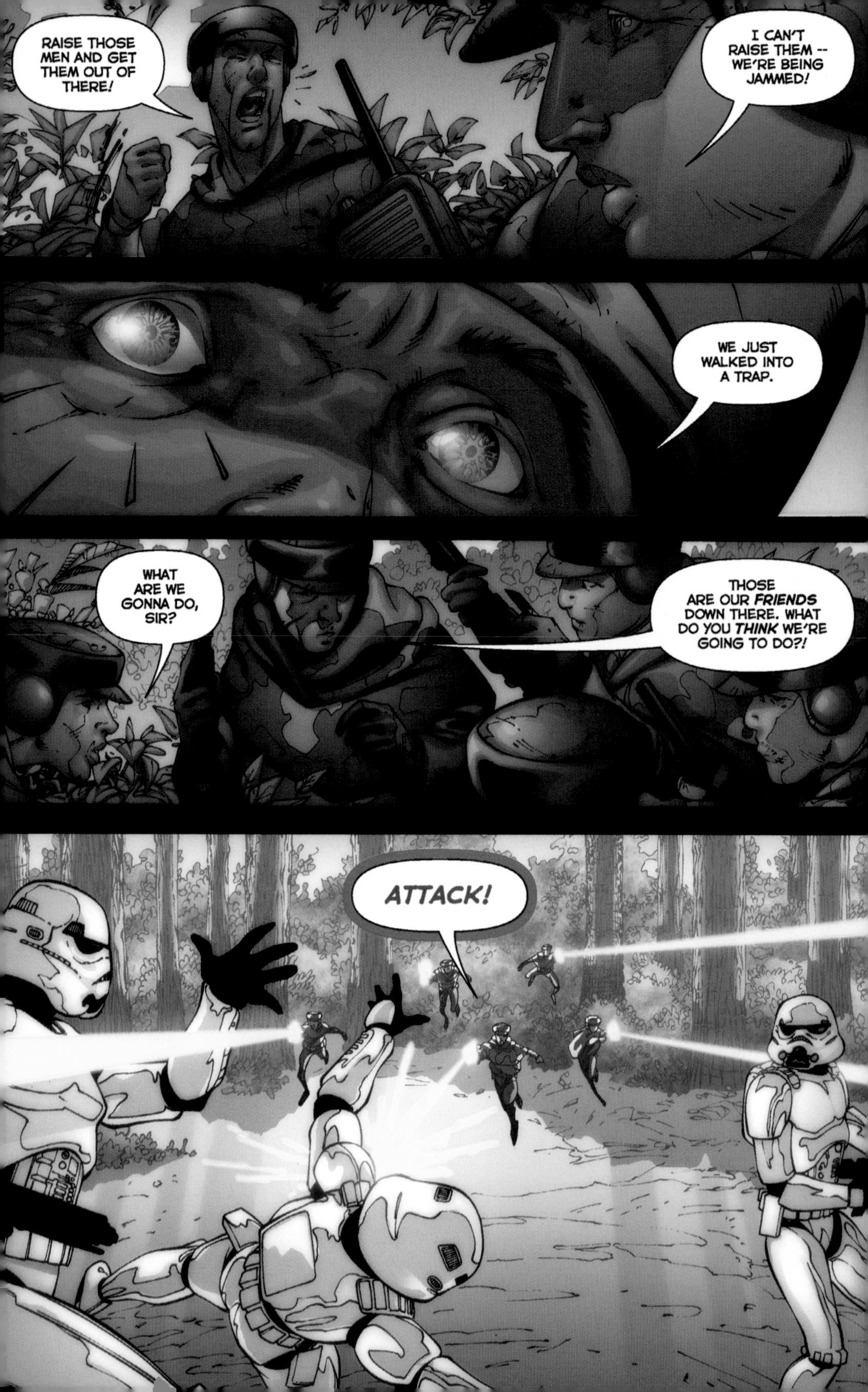
RAISE THOSE MEN AND GET THEM OUT OF THERE!
I CAN'T RAISE THEM -- WE'RE BEING JAMMED!
WE JUST WALKED INTO A TRAP.
WHAT ARE WE GONNA DO, SIR?
THOSE ARE OUR *FRIENDS* DOWN THERE. WHAT DO *YOU THINK* WE'RE GOING TO DO?!
ATTACK!

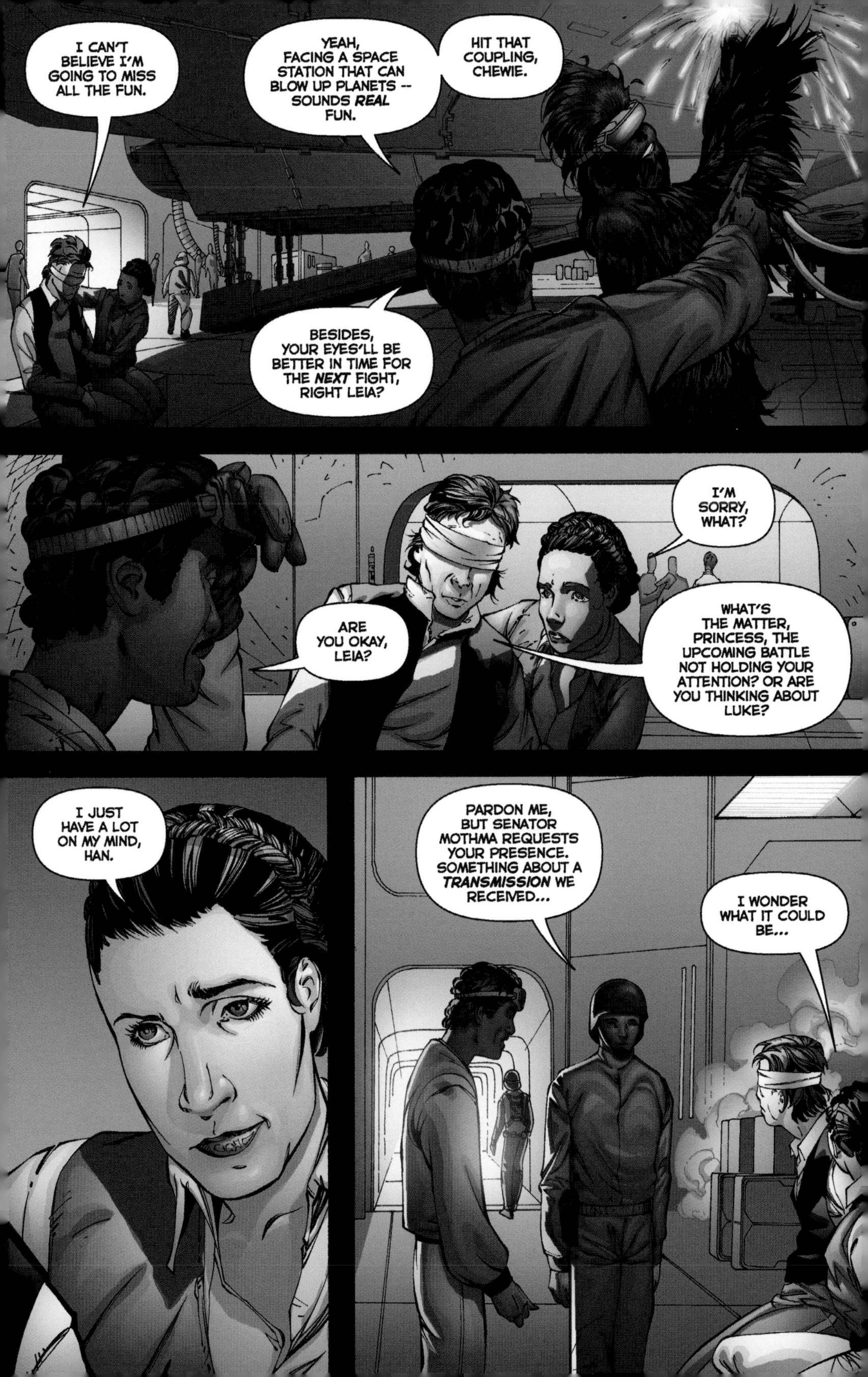
I CAN'T BELIEVE I'M GOING TO MISS ALL THE FUN.
YEAH, FACING A SPACE STATION THAT CAN BLOW UP PLANETS -- SOUNDS *REAL* FUN.
HIT THAT COUPLING, CHEWIE.
BESIDES, YOUR EYES'LL BE BETTER IN TIME FOR THE *NEXT* FIGHT, RIGHT LEIA?
ARE YOU OKAY, LEIA?
I'M SORRY, WHAT?
WHAT'S THE MATTER, PRINCESS, THE UPCOMING BATTLE NOT HOLDING YOUR ATTENTION? OR ARE YOU THINKING ABOUT LUKE?
I JUST HAVE A LOT ON MY MIND, HAN.
PARDON ME, BUT SENATOR MOTHMA REQUESTS YOUR PRESENCE. SOMETHING ABOUT A *TRANSMISSION* WE RECEIVED...
I WONDER WHAT IT COULD BE...

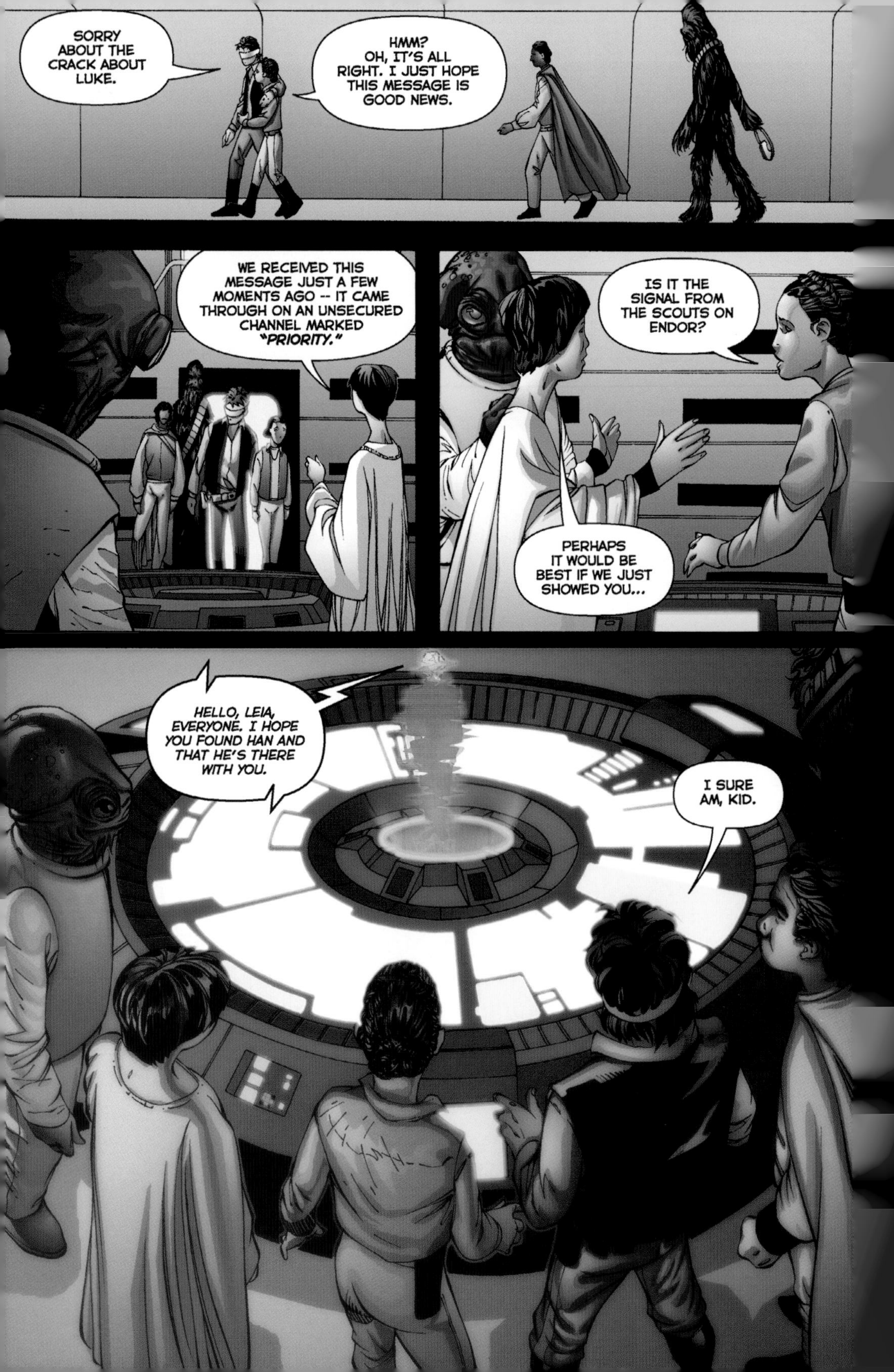
SORRY ABOUT THE CRACK ABOUT LUKE.
HMM? OH, IT'S ALL RIGHT. I JUST HOPE THIS MESSAGE IS GOOD NEWS.
WE RECEIVED THIS MESSAGE JUST A FEW MOMENTS AGO -- IT CAME THROUGH ON AN UNSECURED CHANNEL MARKED "PRIORITY."
IS IT THE SIGNAL FROM THE SCOUTS ON ENDOR?
PERHAPS IT WOULD BE BEST IF WE JUST SHOWED YOU...
HELLO, LEIA, EVERYONE. I HOPE YOU FOUND HAN AND THAT HE'S THERE WITH YOU.
I SURE AM, KID.

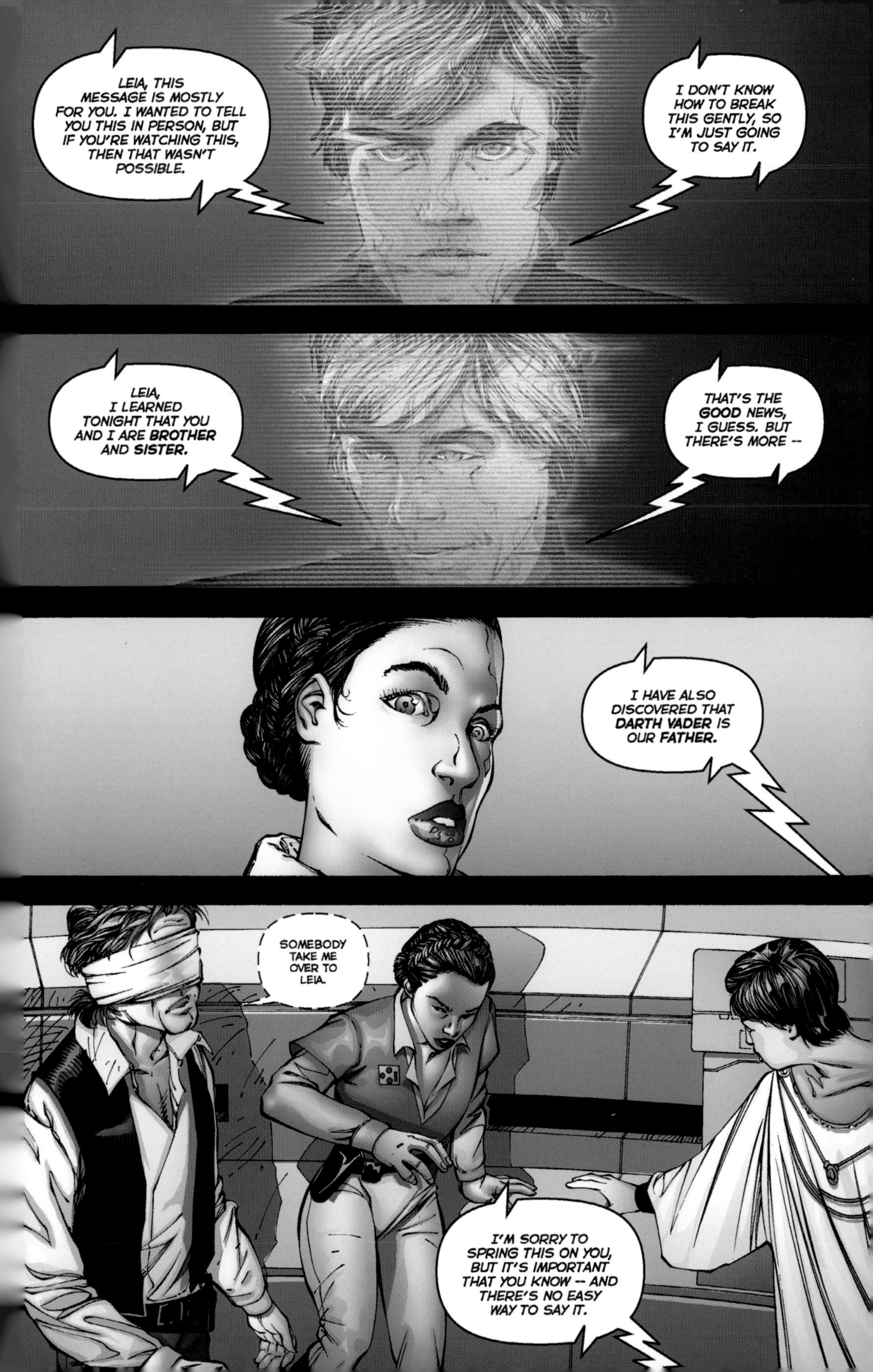
LEIA, THIS MESSAGE IS MOSTLY FOR YOU. I WANTED TO TELL YOU THIS IN PERSON, BUT IF YOU'RE WATCHING THIS, THEN THAT WASN'T POSSIBLE.
I DON'T KNOW HOW TO BREAK THIS GENTLY, SO I'M JUST GOING TO SAY IT.
LEIA, I LEARNED TONIGHT THAT YOU AND I ARE **BROTHER** AND **SISTER.**
THAT'S THE **GOOD** NEWS, I GUESS. BUT THERE'S MORE --
I HAVE ALSO DISCOVERED THAT **DARTH VADER** IS OUR **FATHER.**
SOMEBODY TAKE ME OVER TO LEIA.
I'M SORRY TO SPRING THIS ON YOU, BUT IT'S IMPORTANT THAT YOU KNOW -- AND THERE'S NO EASY WAY TO SAY IT.

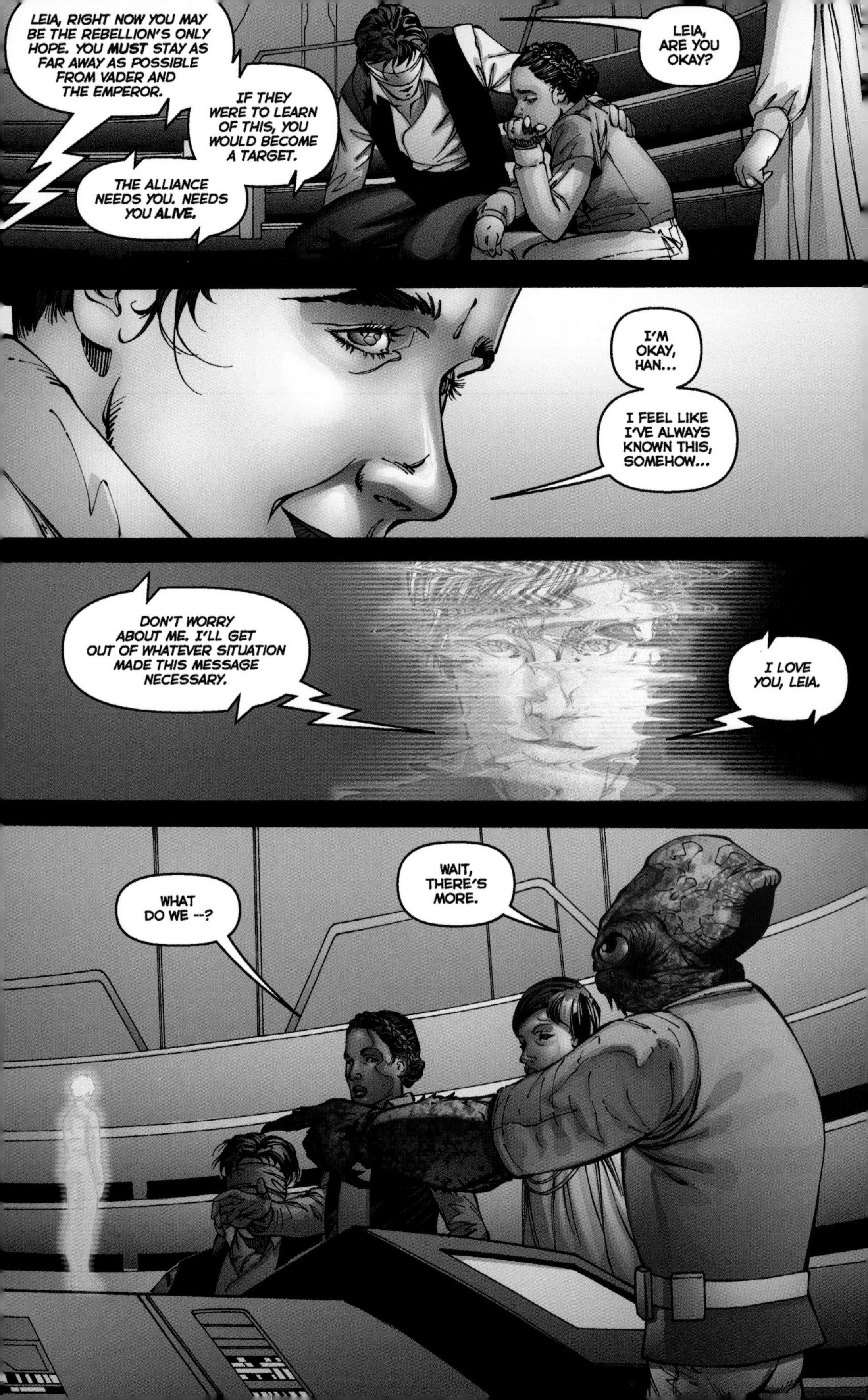
LEIA, RIGHT NOW YOU MAY BE THE REBELLION'S ONLY HOPE. YOU MUST STAY AS FAR AWAY AS POSSIBLE FROM VADER AND THE EMPEROR.
IF THEY WERE TO LEARN OF THIS, YOU WOULD BECOME A TARGET.
THE ALLIANCE NEEDS YOU. NEEDS YOU ALIVE.
LEIA, ARE YOU OKAY?
I'M OKAY, HAN...
I FEEL LIKE I'VE ALWAYS KNOWN THIS, SOMEHOW...
DON'T WORRY ABOUT ME. I'LL GET OUT OF WHATEVER SITUATION MADE THIS MESSAGE NECESSARY.
I LOVE YOU, LEIA.
WHAT DO WE --?
WAIT, THERE'S MORE.

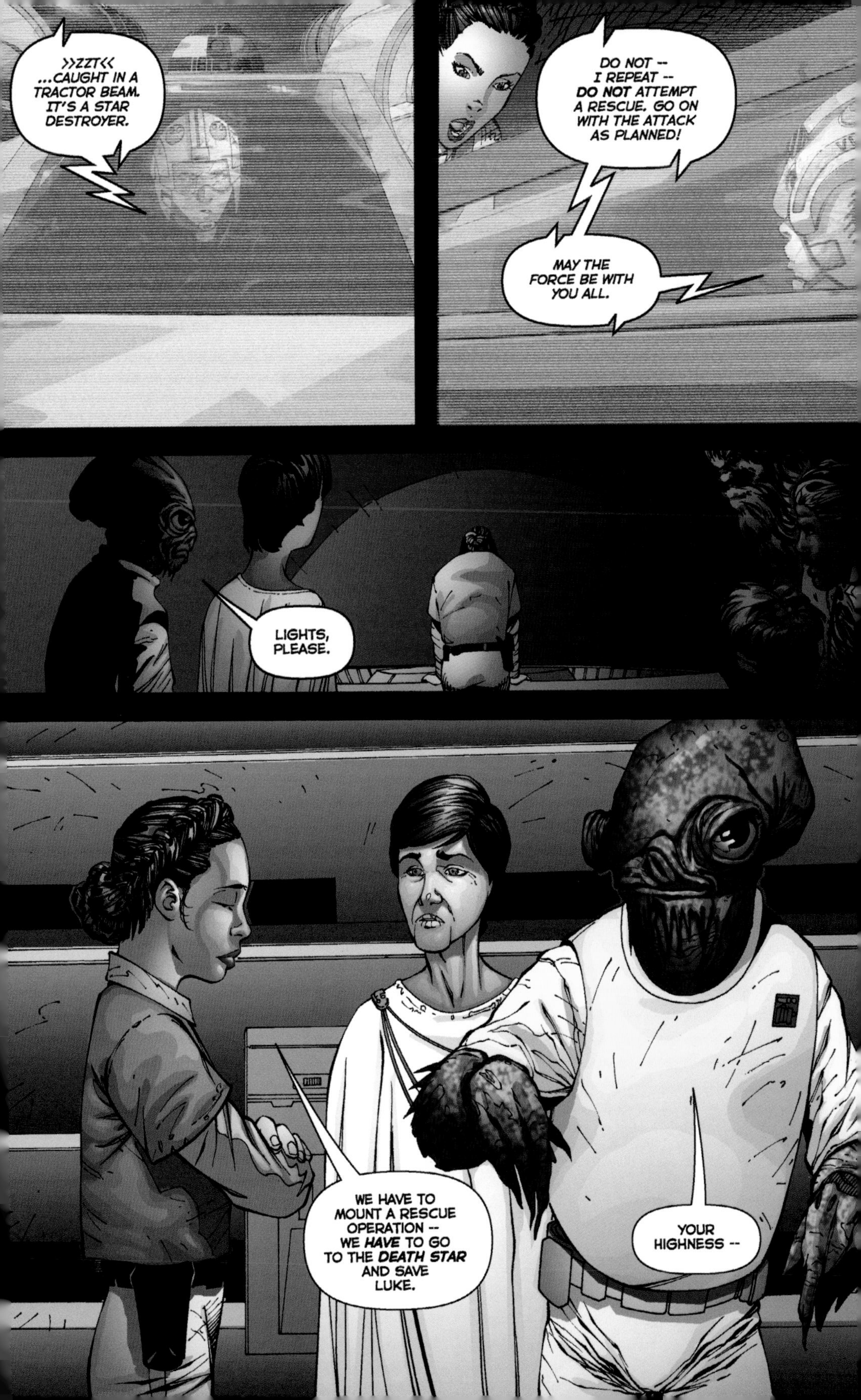
>>ZZT<< ...CAUGHT IN A TRACTOR BEAM. IT'S A STAR DESTROYER.
DO NOT -- I REPEAT -- DO NOT ATTEMPT A RESCUE. GO ON WITH THE ATTACK AS PLANNED!
MAY THE FORCE BE WITH YOU ALL.
LIGHTS, PLEASE.
WE HAVE TO MOUNT A RESCUE OPERATION -- WE HAVE TO GO TO THE DEATH STAR AND SAVE LUKE.
YOUR HIGHNESS --

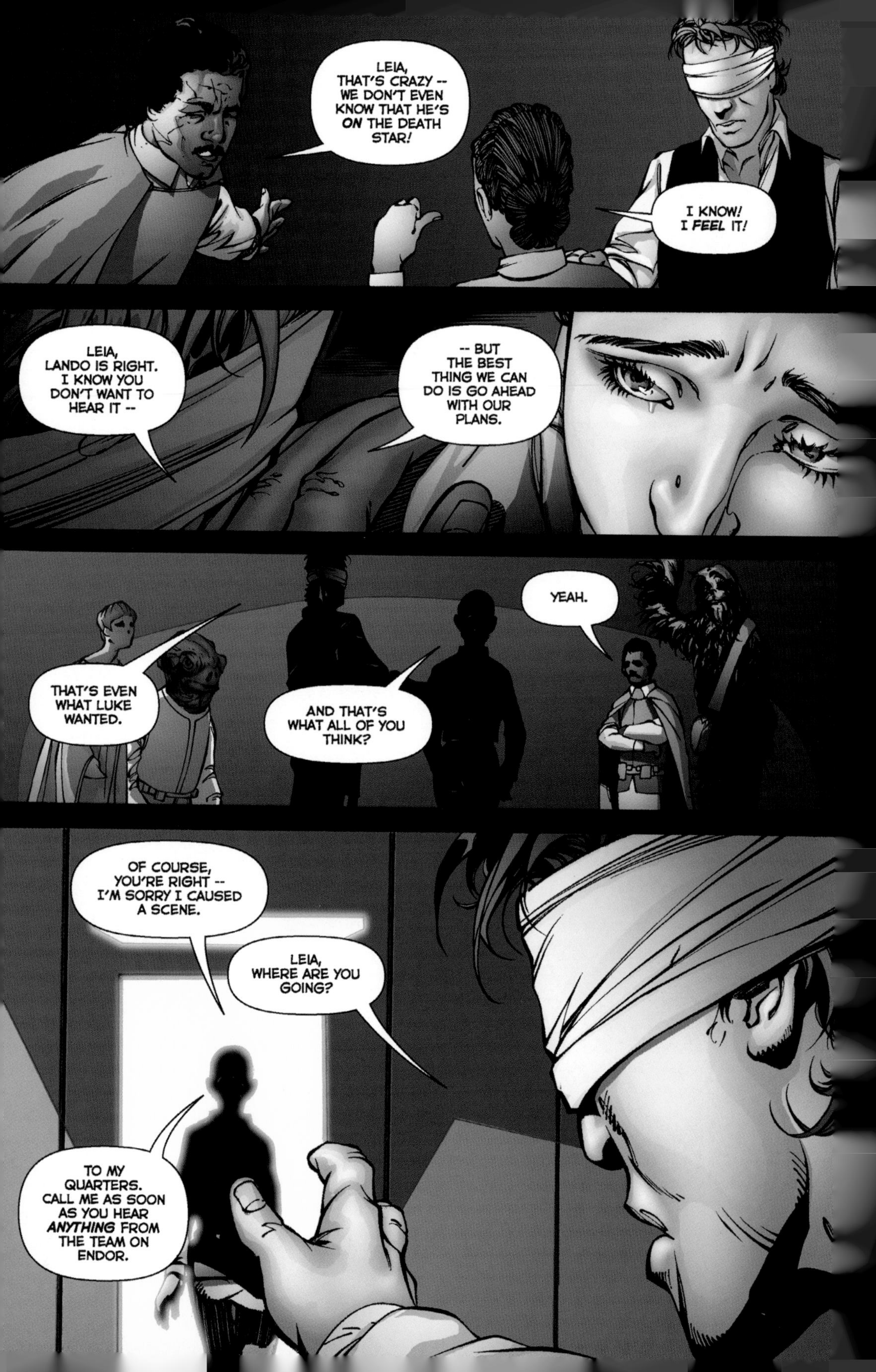
LEIA, THAT'S CRAZY -- WE DON'T EVEN KNOW THAT HE'S *ON* THE DEATH STAR!
I KNOW! I *FEEL* IT!
LEIA, LANDO IS RIGHT. I KNOW YOU DON'T WANT TO HEAR IT --
-- BUT THE BEST THING WE CAN DO IS GO AHEAD WITH OUR PLANS.
THAT'S EVEN WHAT LUKE WANTED.
AND THAT'S WHAT ALL OF YOU THINK?
YEAH.
OF COURSE, YOU'RE RIGHT -- I'M SORRY I CAUSED A SCENE.
LEIA, WHERE ARE YOU GOING?
TO MY QUARTERS. CALL ME AS SOON AS YOU HEAR *ANYTHING* FROM THE TEAM ON ENDOR.

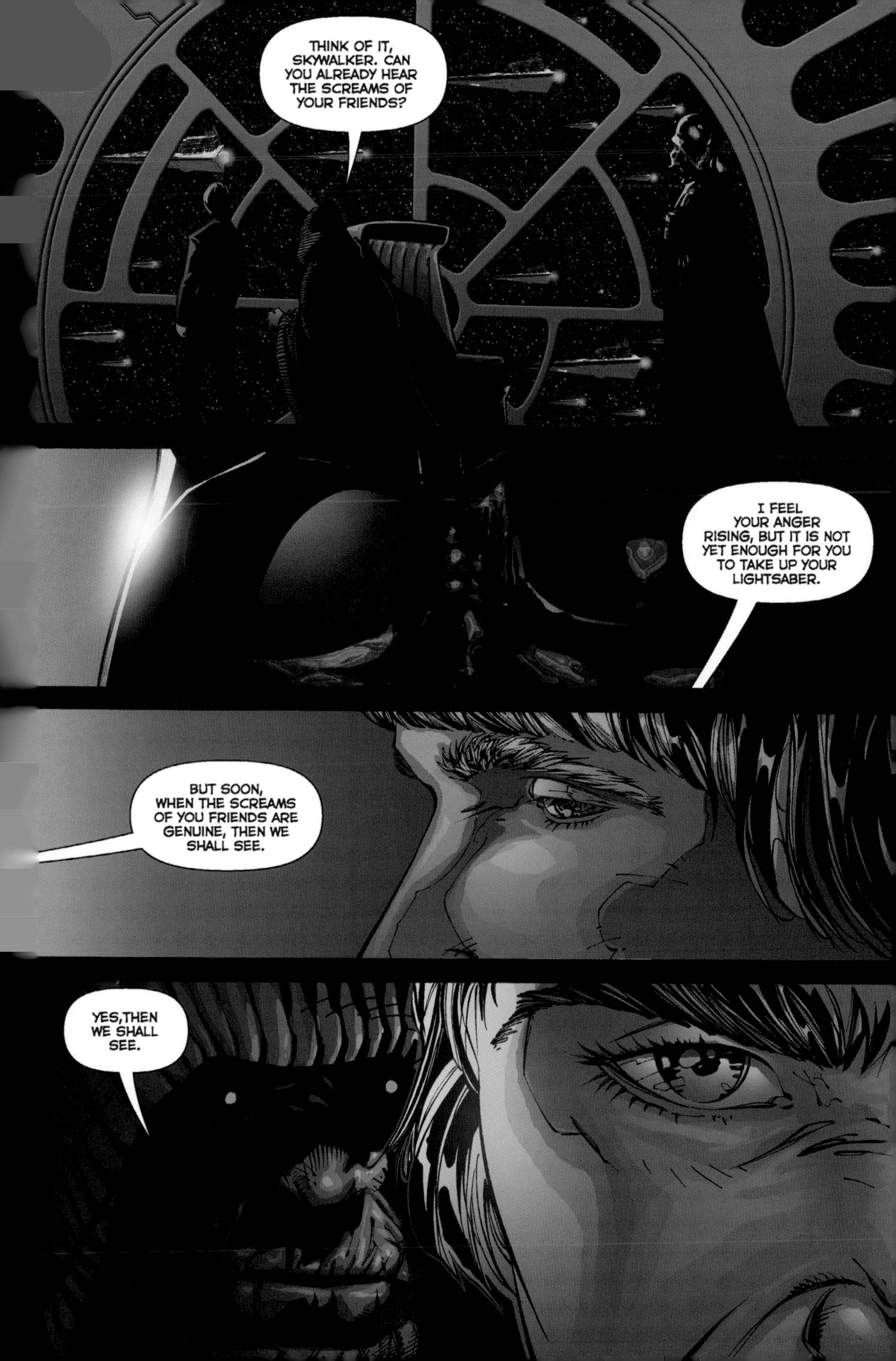
THINK OF IT, SKYWALKER. CAN YOU ALREADY HEAR THE SCREAMS OF YOUR FRIENDS?
I FEEL YOUR ANGER RISING, BUT IT IS NOT YET ENOUGH FOR YOU TO TAKE UP YOUR LIGHTSABER.
BUT SOON, WHEN THE SCREAMS OF YOU FRIENDS ARE GENUINE, THEN WE SHALL SEE.
YES,THEN WE SHALL SEE.

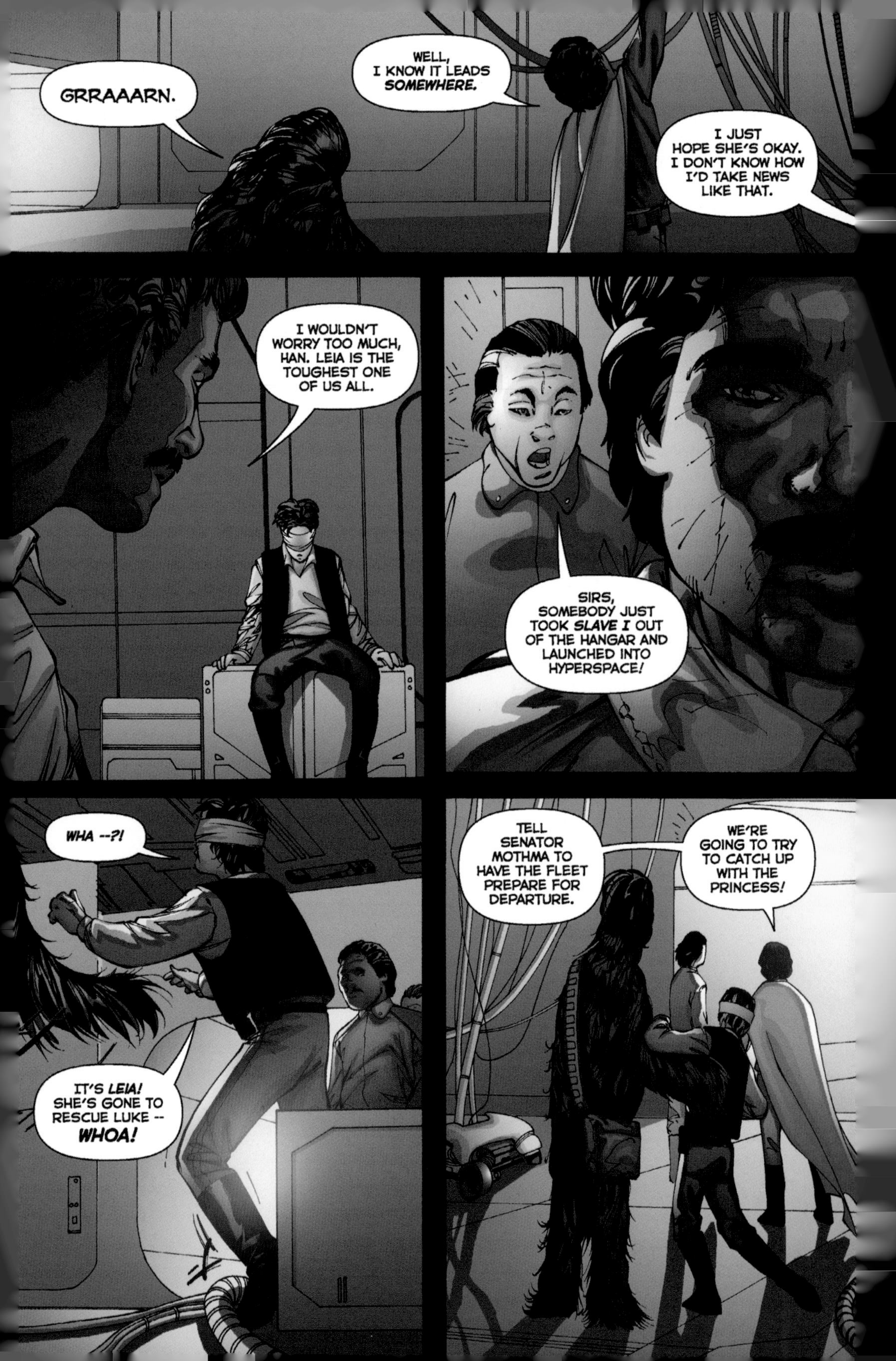
GRRAAARN.
WELL, I KNOW IT LEADS SOMEWHERE.
I JUST HOPE SHE'S OKAY. I DON'T KNOW HOW I'D TAKE NEWS LIKE THAT.
I WOULDN'T WORRY TOO MUCH, HAN. LEIA IS THE TOUGHEST ONE OF US ALL.
SIRS, SOMEBODY JUST TOOK SLAVE I OUT OF THE HANGAR AND LAUNCHED INTO HYPERSPACE!
WHA --?!
IT'S LEIA! SHE'S GONE TO RESCUE LUKE -- WHOA!
TELL SENATOR MOTHMA TO HAVE THE FLEET PREPARE FOR DEPARTURE.
WE'RE GOING TO TRY TO CATCH UP WITH THE PRINCESS!

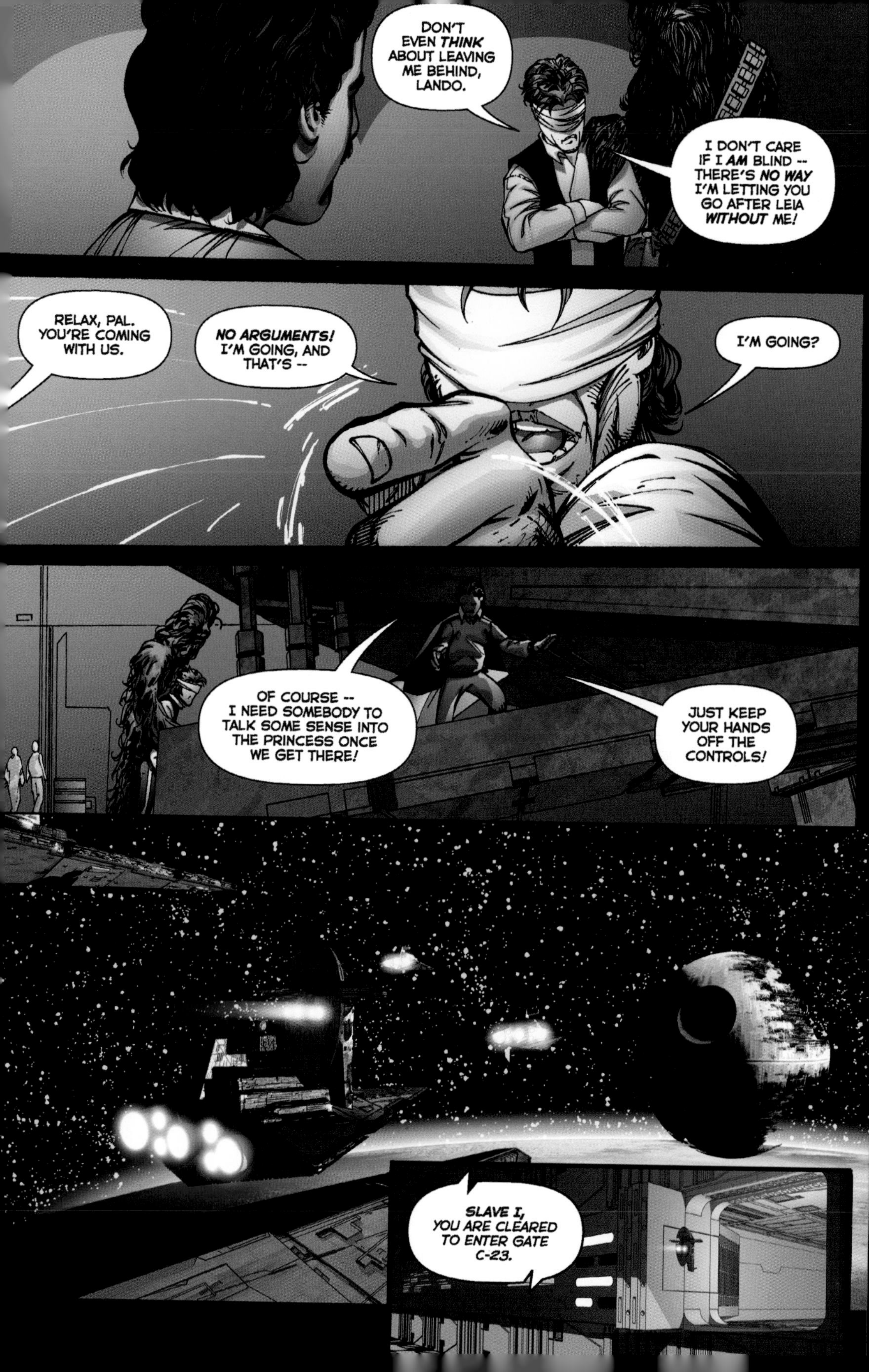
DON'T EVEN *THINK* ABOUT LEAVING ME BEHIND, LANDO.
I DON'T CARE IF I *AM* BLIND -- THERE'S *NO WAY* I'M LETTING YOU GO AFTER LEIA *WITHOUT* ME!
RELAX, PAL. YOU'RE COMING WITH US.
NO ARGUMENTS! I'M GOING, AND THAT'S --
I'M GOING?
OF COURSE -- I NEED SOMEBODY TO TALK SOME SENSE INTO THE PRINCESS ONCE WE GET THERE!
JUST KEEP YOUR HANDS OFF THE CONTROLS!
SLAVE I, YOU ARE CLEARED TO ENTER GATE C-23.

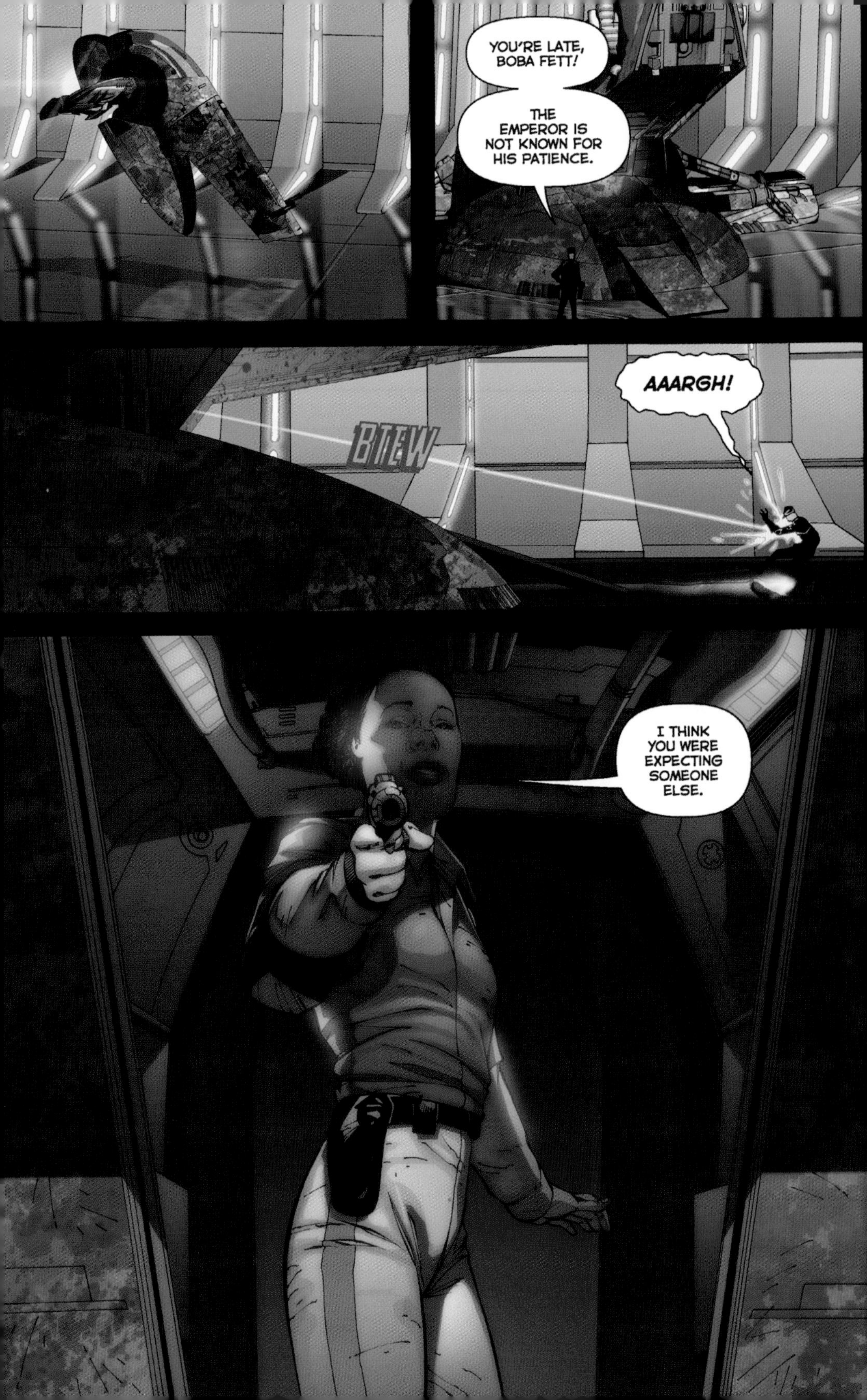
YOU'RE LATE, BOBA FETT!
THE EMPEROR IS NOT KNOWN FOR HIS PATIENCE.
BTEW
AAARGH!
I THINK YOU WERE EXPECTING SOMEONE ELSE.

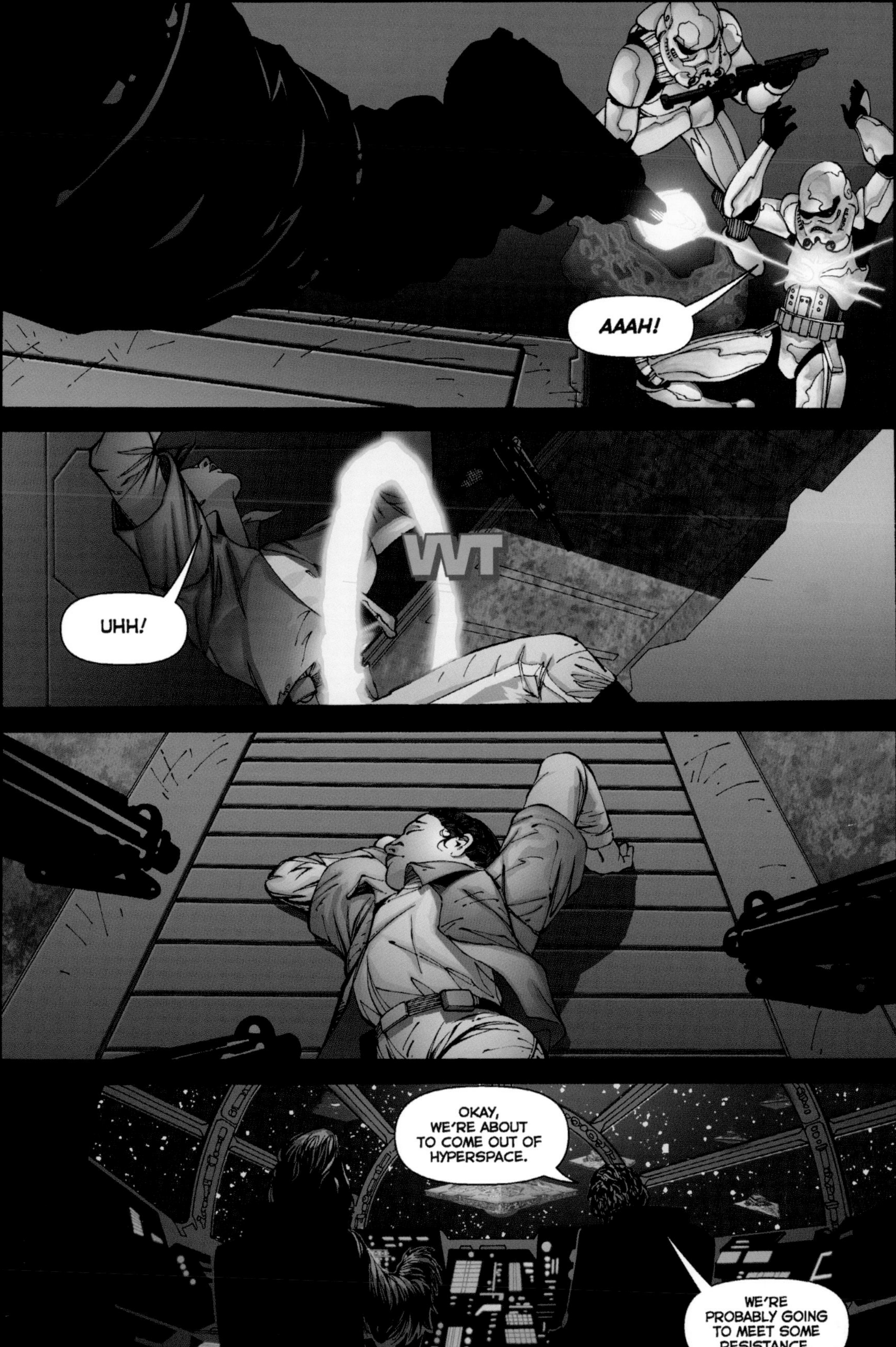
AAAH!
UHH!
VVT
OKAY, WE'RE ABOUT TO COME OUT OF HYPERSPACE.
WE'RE PROBABLY GOING TO MEET SOME RESISTANCE.

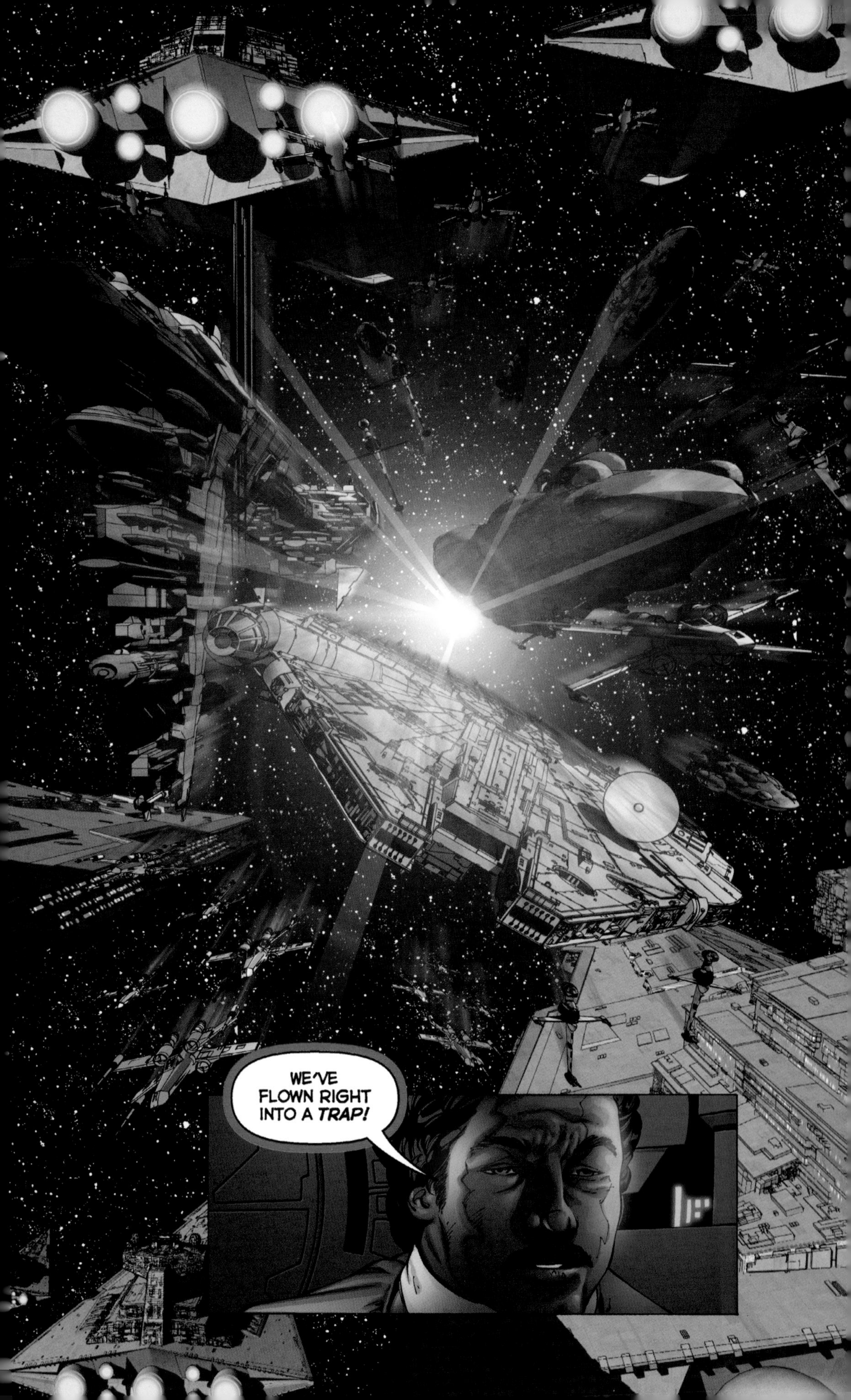
WE'VE FLOWN RIGHT INTO A *TRAP!*

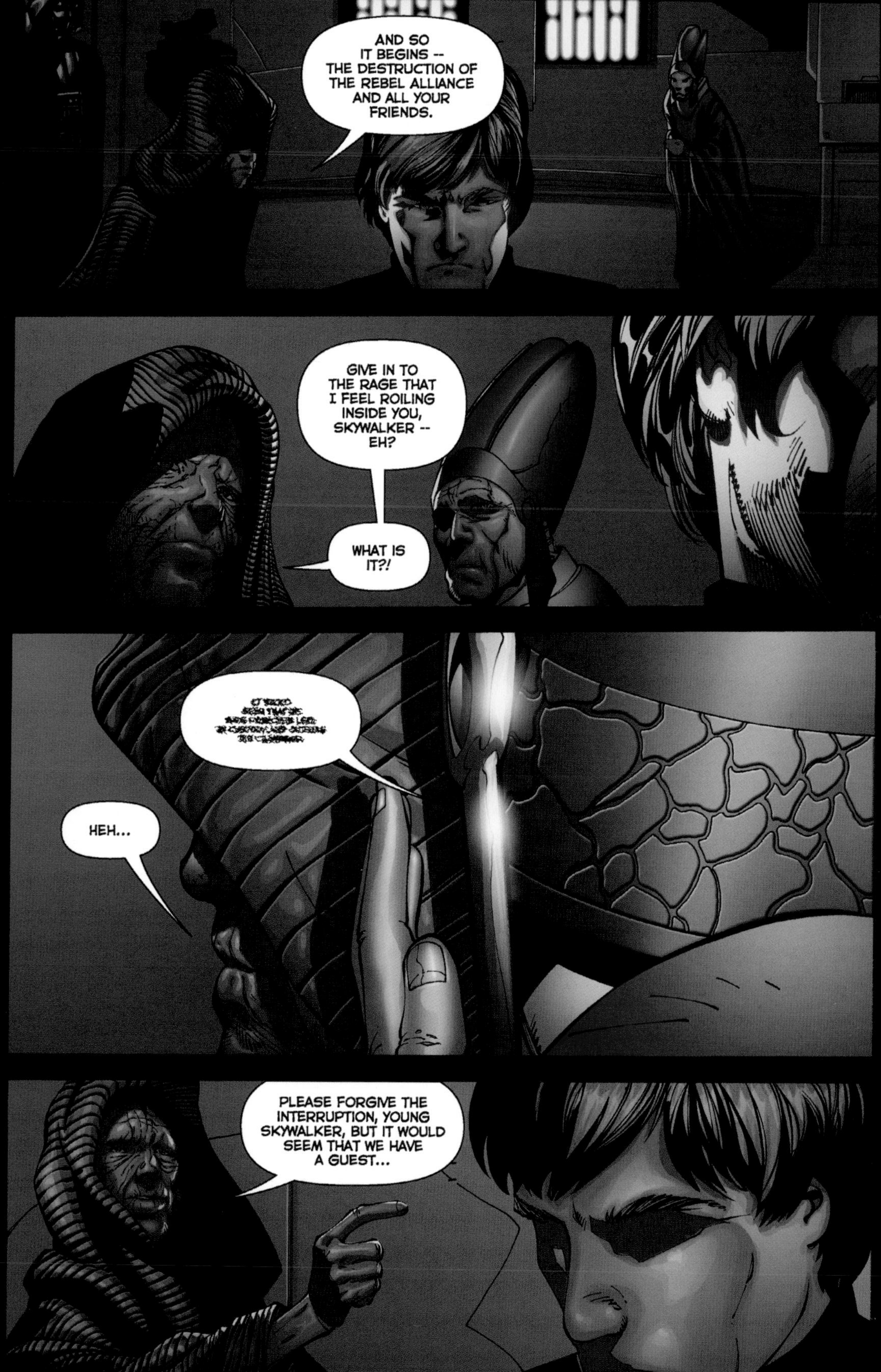
AND SO IT BEGINS -- THE DESTRUCTION OF THE REBEL ALLIANCE AND ALL YOUR FRIENDS.
GIVE IN TO THE RAGE THAT I FEEL ROILING INSIDE YOU, SKYWALKER -- EH?
WHAT IS IT?!
HEH...
PLEASE FORGIVE THE INTERRUPTION, YOUNG SKYWALKER, BUT IT WOULD SEEM THAT WE HAVE A GUEST...

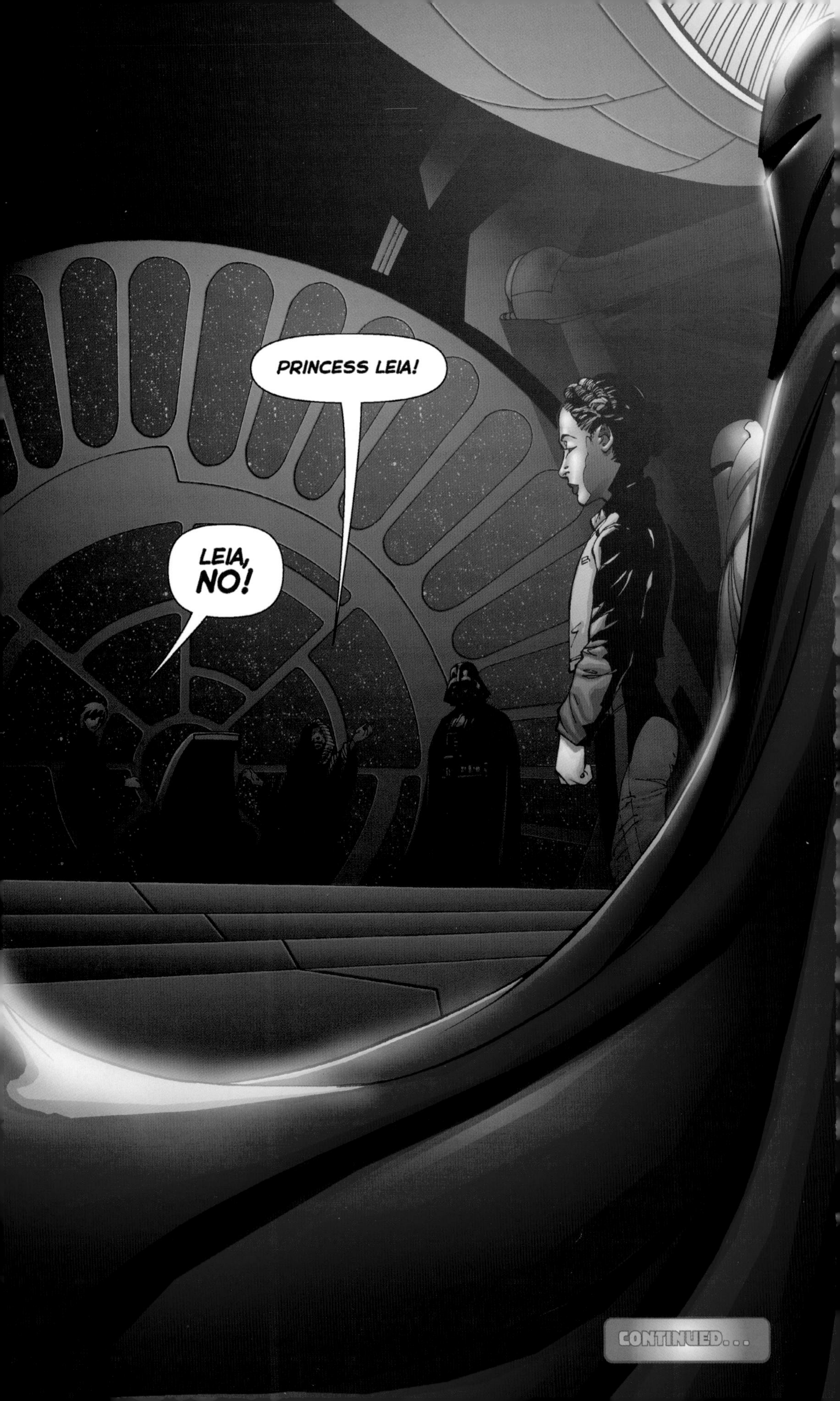
PRINCESS LEIA!
LEIA, NO!
CONTINUED...